The Naked with the Velvet Paws

Dear Eryn~
Just be yourself that's
why people like you!
with Warmest Wishes~
Lisa B. Olek
"13"

Lisa B. Olek
Illustrated by Robin Gruenfelder

Very special thanks go to Elyse and Lauren, my neices, who spent their precious time editing my work.

Also a special shout-out to all the children at Victor Primary and Intermediate Schools for their great suggestions and critiques of my story.

I dedicate this book to my entire family, especially to my sons, David and Devin for all of their encouragement, enthusiasm and love. Also, to my husband, David, for his support and endless hours of assistance and guidance in order to help make my dream come true.

The Naked Cat with the Velvet Paws

Lisa B. Olek

Illustrated by Robin Gruenfelder

Zinger was a handsome black, white, and gray cat with the most beautiful coat anyone had ever seen. It was long and shiny, and had a color pattern that looked like it had been painted by an artist's brush. Zinger was very proud of his handsome appearance, but there was one thing that bothered him more than any other. All of the other cats judged him by his appearance and not by who he really was. When Zinger would walk down the street, he heard cat calls from every corner of the neighborhood.

"Look at him. He thinks he's so great. He struts around like he is king."

"He thinks he's better than everyone else just because of the length of his fur."

"Can't he do something more than take care of his coat. Who would want that ugly coat?"

"If you weren't so ugly, you would be cute."

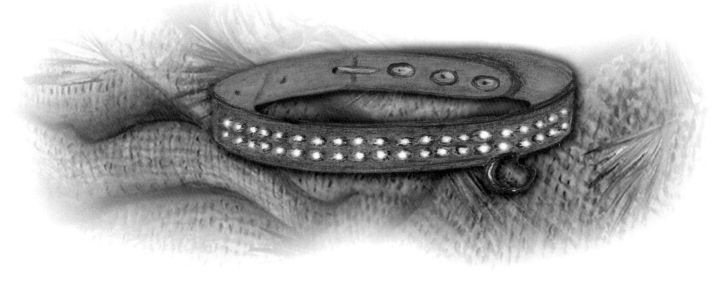

What everyone didn't realize was how sensitive and loving Zinger really was. He didn't take time to work on his coat, nor did he spend hours cleaning and grooming himself. That was just how his fur grew, on its own.

Zinger really wished he could spend time with all kinds of animals and always wanted to be helpful. Instead, he spent many lonely hours, crying himself to sleep because he felt so bullied and unloved by everyone in his neighborhood. He didn't wish to be different and wondered if anyone would ever understand him and like him for who he was on the inside.

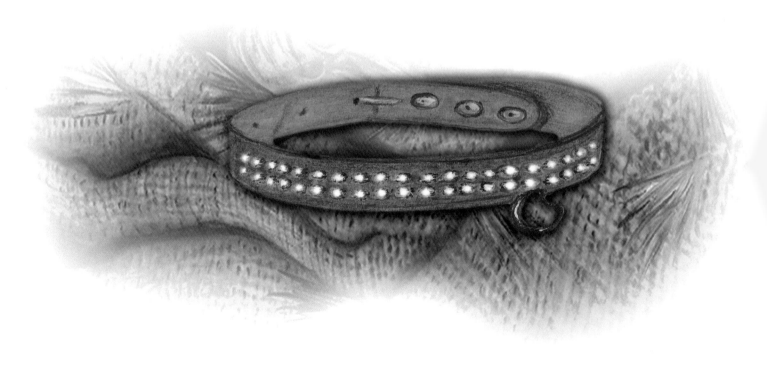

One hot and rainy week, in the middle of August, a terrible storm hit Zinger's community. There was a heavy downpour of rain for almost four days straight. The winds were so strong that a cat could have flown across the yard like a piece of tissue paper flying in the wind. None of the cats would leave their homes. Many of their homes were washed away and there was no food to be found.

Zinger was lucky. He had a very dry spot in a little shed in his owner's backyard. Every day he was given a large bowl of his favorite food and a large, soft, and warm bed to curl up in.

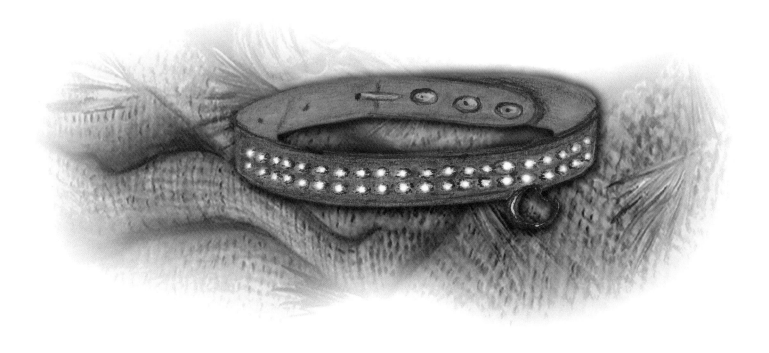

After the storm Zinger ventured out into the world. He could not believe his eyes. Was he in such deep thought about himself that he didn't even hear the storm? His owner's home had its roof ripped off, houses were leveled to the ground, trees were broken in two and lamp posts were twisted in knots. He knew he needed to find a way to help the other cats, so he began to walk the streets to see who he could find.

First he came upon Grandma Cat who had an injured ear. She had lost most of the fur on her head and was shaking from the cold. She was so scared that she was unable to speak at first. Zinger really wasn't sure how he could help her. He cradled her in his arms and spoke softly to her. She sobbed and sobbed and told him she would never be beautiful again and that she had no fur to keep her head warm.

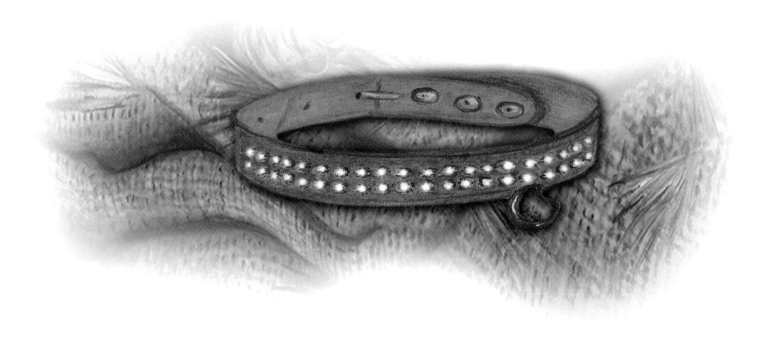

Zinger had a great idea! He laid her gently on the ground and ran back to his shed where he found a pair of scissors, a razor, a bottle of glue, and an old burlap bag.

He quickly ran back to Grandma Cat, sat next to her and told her that she had nothing to worry about. Zinger took the razor and shaved every last hair off the top of his head. He trimmed the fur to match the length of her fur. Then he carefully cut the burlap into a hat and glued his fur to the burlap.

He gave her the most gorgeous fur hat she had ever seen. Grandma Cat was so proud of her new head of fur. She gently grabbed Zinger's paw and held his soft, white, velvet foot in her quivering paw and said, "Thank you so much for helping me. I have never met such a selfless cat in my life. Thank you for being so sweet and gentle to an old cat like me."

Zinger's heart felt so good he thought it might burst.

Zinger left Grandma Cat's side and walked three blocks down the road. As he walked passed a tiny dark alley he heard a shrill, "MEOW! HELP!"

He slowly crept into the alley not knowing if it was safe. There, he came across a beautiful Persian cat with fur as gray as a storm sky. His beautiful, full, bushy tail was trapped by a large cinder block which had fallen from the drugstore roof.

Zinger tried as hard as he could to lift the block but he couldn't get it to budge. He grabbed the scissors and used them to pry the block from the cat's tail. After several tries his tail was finally free. As Gray Cat removed his tail he realized the fur was all scraped off and his tail was crimped in two places. It looked like the letter "Z".

Gray Cat was so upset that he didn't know what to do. Zinger had a great thought though. He took the burlap and cut out the shape of the cat's tail. He stuffed it with the extra burlap and a stick that was laying on the ground. Then Zinger took the razor and shaved the fur off of his own beautiful gray tail. He carefully covered the burlap with fur and trimmed it so that it looked exactly like Gray Cat's bushy tail. He told Gray Cat to cover his eyes because he had a BIG surprise for him.

Zinger then took the newly crafted tail and carefully straightened Gray Cat's crooked tail and slipped it into the tail he had just made. On the count of three he had Gray Cat open his eyes. He could not believe his big bushy, straight tail. It was more beautiful than it had ever been before! He asked Zinger how he had done it and Zinger just replied, "A cat as beautiful as you deserves to have a beautiful tail."

When Zinger stood up to leave, Gray Cat was shocked to see Zinger's tail. Not one bit of fur on it. He looked at Zinger with tears in his eyes. He said, "Zinger, you are the most caring cat I have ever met. You truly have a heart of gold."

Zinger turned to Gray Cat and said, "It was the least I could do. You need a beautiful, full, bushy tail more than I do."

Gray Cat was so overwhelmed by Zinger's generous act that he began to cry. He couldn't believe how nice Zinger was to him considering he had been bullying him for so many years. He even got all the other cats involved in his mean antics. Zinger never thought he would see Gray Cat come to tears and be thanking him. He gathered his things and said a quick goodbye. As he left, Gray Cat continued to admire his beautiful, full, gray, bushy tail and Zinger was gently wiping a tear from his own eye.

Onward Zinger went. He trudged through fields of debris, over furniture and old photos, as well as people's shoes and clothes. He was so sad that he sobbed with every step he took. Soon it began to get dark and Zinger decided it was time to turn back and go home. When he was only a few blocks from his shed, he heard tiny cries in the silence of the evening. He followed these cries to an overturned car where he found six tiny kittens hiding underneath it. Zinger slowly approached them so he would not frighten them. He was also unsure if the mother or father was around. After scoping out the situation he realized that no one was there with the kittens, so he asked them where their mom and dad were. They said, "Mom went to find food, but we have not seen our dad for a long time. We're so scared, we just want our mommy."

The poor little kittens were soaked from the rain and were very cold and hungry. They did not have their mom there to keep them warm.

Zinger once again took his razor and shaved the fur off of his back and legs. He carefully glued it to the burlap and made a blanket for them. He gently laid the blanket over the kittens, tucked them in and stayed until they fell asleep. He then made his way home to his little shed.

Zinger never realized how fortunate he was to be surrounded by a family who loved him and a good warm home to live in. For the first time he knew he couldn't spend so much time letting the bullies in the community hurt his heart. He realized he was a beautiful cat on the inside as well as the outside.

Zinger no longer had any fur left on his body or head, just on his paws, nose and ears, but he didn't care. He finally realized what was important, that he was the most beautiful cat in the land, not because of his fur, but for what was in his heart. Zinger was very thankful for all he had and was so exhausted, he fell asleep.

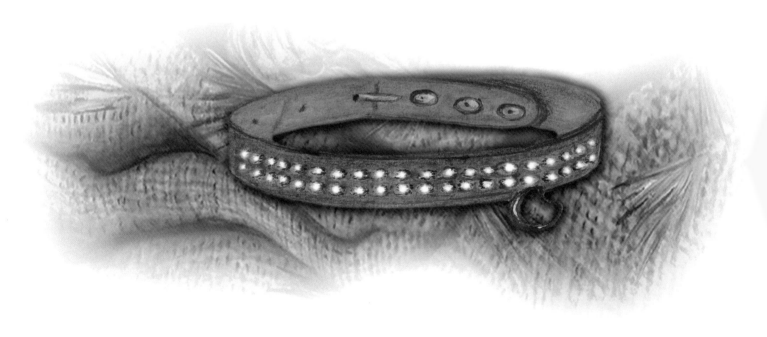

Zinger

After the storm, the cats in the community looked at Zinger in a different way. They felt badly for bullying him. They felt guilty that he no longer had any fur to keep him warm. He had put everyone else first without thinking of himself.

All of the cats in the community were called together to meet in the alley where Gray Cat had his accident. Every cat agreed that they needed to honor Zinger for his brave acts of kindness and they swore that they would never bully anyone again.

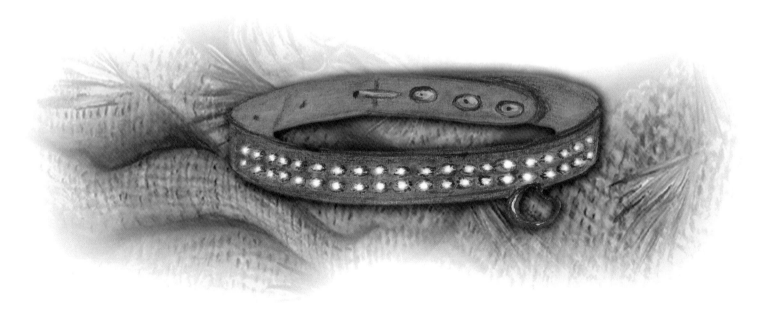

Gray Cat stood on the very cinder block that had crushed his tail and exclaimed, "We're all gathered here to honor our own hero, Zinger. Without consideration to his own safety, he gave up his fur to help others. Zinger, it is my honor to present you with this red velvet rhinestone collar. It has one rhinestone for each cat and kitten in this community. May it always remind you of how much we appreciate you for being a special cat. More importantly, may its sparkle and shine remind all of us, that it's not the fur that makes the cat, but the heart that lies beneath."

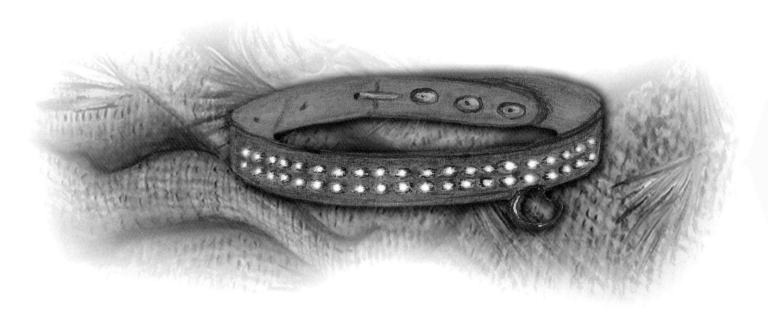

Now Zinger proudly walks the bully free streets of his community, hairless as hairless can be, with his red velvet rhinestone collar shining brightly. Zinger is very proud to be known as "The Naked Cat with the Velvet Paws!"

pg. 32

Zinger's Anti-Bullying Club

I, _____ agree to join with Zinger to stamp out bullying, both at school and outside of school.

I believe that no one deserves to be bullied and that every one regardless of race, color, religion, size and gender, popularity, athletic, academic or social ability or intelligence has the right to feel safe, secure and respected in and out of school as well as at play and at sporting events.

I agree to:
 Not call someone a name.
 Not make up stories about someone.
 Not make faces or bad gestures towards others.
 Not partake in any actions that are likely to make
   someone feel badly about themselves.
 Not hit shove, spit or kick anyone.
 Not laugh at or make fun of someone.
 Not exclude others from play.

I will also agree to the following :
 To treat others with respect and kindness.
 Help others who have been bullied.
 Tell a teacher, parent or an adult if bullying does occur.
 Not let myself get involved with bullying.
 To always try my best to be a good role model for others.

Signed by: _____

Date: _____

Zinger's Anti-Bullying Club for the Little Kittens

I pledge that I will try my best to be a good example to all the kids I meet by:

Never calling names.

Never making up stories about someone.

Never making faces or bad expressions towards anyone.

By Dan Olek

I was born in 1956 in McKeesport, PA. I grew up with a sister and two brothers. My mother loved animals and passed that love and compassion on to all of us. We always had cats and a dog in our home, each one touching our lives in a different way.

My husband and I both share the love of all kind of animals. My two boys, David and Devin, had many animals in their childhood including snakes, tortoises, turtles, hamsters, rats, fish, miniature opossum, birds and dogs. The one animal missing was a cat. My husband was allergic to cats, but he always promised me if we found a hairless one, he would buy it for me.

Five years ago we went to buy our son a new puppy. While we were selecting her, the breeder brought out a hairless kitten. As they say the rest is history. We came home with not only a dog but a new hairless kitten named Zinger.

Zinger was a huge inspiration for this book. He is so different from any cat I have ever owned, not only in his looks but his personality. As I watched friends and strangers reactions to Zinger, it opened my eyes to how we judge not only people, but also animals by their looks. I hope this book inspires children to understand that it is not someone's looks, but the love and compassion in their heart that makes this world a better place.

CPSIA information can be obtained
at www.ICGtesting.com
Printed in the USA
LVIW020755220313
325349LV00004B

9 781601 310941